MARY-KATE AND ASHLEY in ACTION!

The Music Meltdown

A novelization by Judy Katschke
based on the teleplay
by Robin Riordan

📖 HarperEntertainment
An Imprint of HarperCollins*Publishers*

A PARACHUTE PRESS BOOK

D0669146

A PARACHUTE PRESS BOOK

Parachute Publishing, L.L.C.
156 Fifth Avenue, Suite 302
New York, NY 10010

Published by
HarperEntertainment
An Imprint of HarperCollins*Publishers*
10 East 53rd Street, New York, NY 10022

ISBN 0-06-009307-2

HarperCollins®, ®, and HarperEntertainment™ are trademarks of HarperCollins Publishers Inc.

First printing: June 2003

Printed in China

Visit the on-line book boutique on the World Wide Web at
www.mary-kateandashley.com.

Visit HarperEntertainment on the World Wide Web at
www.harpercollins.com

10 9 8 7 6 5 4 3 2 1

CHAPTER ONE
Sounds Like Trouble

"Peppermint Pink is definitely my favorite color," Ashley said. She looked at her fingernails. She was sitting on her bedroom floor.

Mary-Kate waved her hands in the air. "Our nails should be dry soon," she said.

"Then we can hit the library," Ashley said, "to study for our science test."

Mary-Kate nodded. "You know, it's nice to do normal stuff like this every once in a while," she said.

"Totally!" Ashley agreed.

Mary-Kate's and Ashley's lives were anything *but* normal. The teenagers were special agents. They worked for a top-secret organization that fought crime. Their missions took them all over the world.

"We are going to learn everything there is to know about the science of sound," Ashley said. "Then we'll ace our test."

"Speaking of sound—listen to this!" Mary-Kate exclaimed. She jumped up and ran across the room to her stereo. "I love this song!"

"Polyester Pal!" Ashley cried. "That's my favorite group. Pump it up, Mary-Kate!"

Mary-Kate turned up the volume. She and Ashley began dancing.

"What's going on?" a voice yelled over the music. Ashley turned and saw their Scottish terrier, Quincy, in the doorway.

Quincy looked like an ordinary dog. But he was really a super-robot! He helped the girls on all their missions.

"Quincy!" Mary-Kate cried. She grabbed his front paws and lifted him up on his hind legs.

Quincy shook his tail back and forth.

"Go, Quincy! Go, Quincy!" Ashley cheered.

SCREEEECH! A horrible sound came out of the speakers.

"Huh?" Mary-Kate asked.

The radio went silent. A second later it pumped out a loud techno-beat.

Mary-Kate turned some of the radio controls. "What happened to our song?" she asked.

"I don't think it's the radio," Ashley said. "The same thing happened at the mall yesterday, remember? The song that was playing just stopped."

"Right!" Mary-Kate nodded. "And the song that took over was the same awful song that's playing right now. I think it's a new single by some guy named Capital D."

"That's weird," Ashley said. "I wonder if—"

BEEP! BEEP! Ashley glanced down at her wrist. She was getting a message through her special-agent bracelet. The

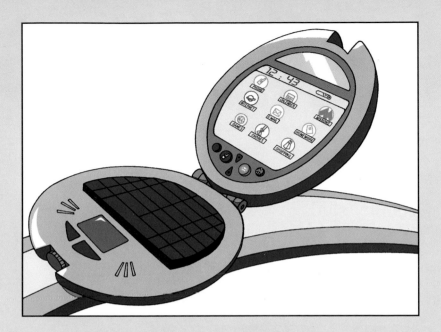

bracelet was a computer and telephone all in one!

"It's Headquarters," Ashley told Mary-Kate.

"And it's code red!" Mary-Kate said, looking down at her own watch. "This could be serious."

"Studying will have to wait," Ashley said. "We're off to save the world."

Mary-Kate smiled. "Again!"

CHAPTER TWO

Where in the World Is Capital D?

"Thanks for picking us up, Rod," Ashley said.

"Don't mention it," seventeen-year-old Rodney Choy said. He worked for Headquarters, too. Rod drove the girls wherever they needed to go.

"Looks like we have a big problem," Rod went on. "Someone is messing with radio stations and DJs all across the country."

"Tell us about it." Mary-Kate groaned. "We can't get any music on the radio except some horrible song by Capital D."

"If you ask me," Quincy said, "Capital D is a Capital Dork!"

"I hope we can take care of this mission fast," Ashley said. "Mary-Kate and I have a big science test coming up."

"What is it on?" Rod asked.

"Sound," Ashley said.

"I know tons of facts about sound," Quincy said. "Sound travels in waves through the air at different levels."

"Those levels are called frequencies, right?" Mary-Kate asked.

"Right," Quincy said.

"Yes!" Mary-Kate cheered. "I can feel an A already."

"High-frequency waves have high-pitched sounds," Quincy went on. "Low-frequency waves have low-pitched sounds."

"We didn't even have to go to the library," Ashley said. "Quincy can tell us everything we need to know!"

"Here's some more info," Quincy said. "High-frequency is much stronger and faster than low-frequency. In fact—"

SCREEECH!

"Oh, no," Mary-Kate said. "Not again!"

The Jeep's radio went silent. Then a Capital D song blasted from the speakers.

Quincy dived under the car seat. "This music is so bad, it hurts my ears!" he whined.

"I'd better step on it," Rod said. He steered the Jeep up a ramp and into Mary-Kate and Ashley's private jet.

Inside the jet was fifteen-year-old Ivan Quintero. He invented high-tech gadgets for the girls to use. He had even invented Quincy!

"What's up, IQ?" Ashley asked. IQ was Ivan's nickname.

"*This* is what's up," IQ said. He pointed to a photo of a tall man with wild blond hair on his computer screen.

"So that is Capital D," Mary-Kate said.

"Capital D records his own music," IQ explained. "His company is in Washington, D.C."

"So why is he forcing everyone to listen to his songs?" Ashley asked.

"Capital D is totally in love with himself," IQ explained. "He doesn't want anyone to listen to any other music but his."

"That's awful!" Ashley said.

"It's up to you to find out how he's controlling the airwaves," IQ said. "And figure out how to stop him."

He pointed to a map of the United States on his computer screen. "There are only three dance clubs left in the country that can play their own music," he explained. "Every place else can only play Capital D's songs!"

Mary-Kate and Ashley looked at the screen. Three red lights flashed on the map.

Two were in New York. One was in Washington, D.C.

"You'll have to hurry," Rod added. "A global peace meeting starts tomorrow in Washington, D.C. There's going to be a big party with lots of music."

"Throughout the night, they're going to play the national anthem of every country at the meeting," IQ went on. "Think of

what would happen if the anthems got cut off."

"That could really upset some world leaders," Ashley said. "And ruin our chances for world peace!"

"Now do you see why Headquarters wanted their two best agents on the job?" IQ asked.

Ashley nodded. "Looks like we're off to our nation's capital—to catch Capital D!"

CHAPTER THREE
Rockin' the House

Ashley climbed into the cockpit of the jet. She took the controls.

Mary-Kate sat next to her. She began typing on a laptop computer.

"Posing as DJs is a great idea, Mary-Kate—I mean, Sister Scarlet," Ashley

said, using Mary-Kate's DJ name. She lifted the jet into the air. "No one will think we are special agents."

"Thanks, Amber Jammer!" Mary-Kate said. "Not only will it get us into the clubs, but we get to wear funky clothes like these!"

Mary-Kate showed off her baggy jeans, tiny T-shirt, and platform sneakers.

"And wait until you see the ad I'm creating for us on the Web," Mary-Kate went on. "It's going to make us look like the hottest DJs in D.C.!"

"Hot enough for the Funk Factory to let us spin tonight?" Ashley asked. The Funk Factory was the club in D.C. that could still play their own music.

"You know it!" Mary-Kate replied.

Rod came into the cockpit. "IQ and I thought you might like a hip-hop dog to help you."

Ashley turned her head. Rod was holding Quincy. And Quincy did *not* look happy.

His fur was dyed bright blue. He was dressed in a fake leopard-print doggy coat and spiked collar.

"You look so—" Ashley started.

"Ridiculous?" Quincy yelled. "Stupid? Clownlike?"

"Cool!" Ashley finished. "With a Capital C."

"As long as we're talking about cool,"

Mary-Kate put in. "How cool are these X-ray headbands that IQ made us?"

Ashley shook her head. "Mary-Kate, the only reason you are a special agent is because of the toys!" she said.

"That's not true," Mary-Kate said. "The best part of the job is helping people." She paused. "But the toys don't hurt, either!"

Ashley giggled.

Mary-Kate pulled the X-ray headband over her eyes. She stared at Quincy. "Wow! I can see inside your body. With all your wires, you look like the inside of a television set!" she exclaimed.

Quincy shook out his blue fur. "At this point," he said, "I probably look better on the inside than on the outside!"

"These headbands are awesome," Ashley said.

"And we're going to use them to crack this case wide open!" Mary-Kate cheered.

"Hey, Funk Factory!" Mary-Kate shouted into the microphone. "This is Sister Scarlet. Amber Jammer and I are going to turn this club into a major dance party!"

It was Mary-Kate and Ashley's first night as DJs. Ashley pushed a few buttons on the DJ equipment. Polyester Pal boomed through the speakers.

The girls jumped in front of the booth and grooved to the beat. Even Quincy got

into the act. He started dancing on his hind legs!

The crowd cheered and clapped. Everyone was having a great time! But then—

SCREEECH!

The music stopped. A second later a horrible song by Capital D blared out of the speakers!

The crowd started to boo.

"Hey, what happened to the music?" one dancer called out.

Ashley turned to Mary-Kate. "Looks like Capital D is in the house," she said.

Mary-Kate nodded. "I'm going to check out the sound equipment."

"And I'll look through the crowd for anybody that looks strange," Ashley said.

Mary-Kate walked away.

Ashley scanned the floor of the dance club. All the dancers were covering their

ears—except for one person. A boy in the middle of the floor was smiling and bopping to the beat.

He's the one I should be talking to, Ashley thought. She squeezed through the crowd and made her way toward the boy.

"You must be a fan of Capital D," Ashley said.

The boy stopped dancing. "D is

awesome!" he said. "He makes the greatest music. He and I work together."

"So you're Capital D's friend?" Ashley asked.

"I'm Sammy Sam, his main man!" he said.

Ashley's eyes lit up. Maybe Sammy Sam could help her meet Capital D!

"My sister and I are *huge* fans," Ashley fibbed. "You couldn't introduce us to him, could you?"

Sammy Sam looked at Ashley. He didn't seem to trust her. "If you're really a fan," he said, "what's the name of the first song Capital D ever wrote?"

Ashley gulped. She had no idea! "Ummm," she said. "The one where . . . uh . . ."

Sammy Sam shook his head. "You're not a real fan!" he said.

"Me?" Ashley cried. "I—"

"Whoops! I guess I was wrong about you," Sammy Sam said.

Huh? Ashley thought.

"'Me, I, It's All About Me!' That's the name of the song!" Sammy Sam finished.

Am I lucky or what? Ashley thought. She took a few steps away from Sammy Sam. She flipped open her special-agent bracelet.

"How's it going, Mary-Kate?" she said into the bracelet.

"Not so great!" Mary-Kate replied. "There are so many wires back here. I feel like I'm walking around in spaghetti!"

"I have some news that will cheer you up," Ashley said. "Guess which two special agents are about to meet Capital D?"

CHAPTER FOUR
No Way Out

"Here is a picture of me after a swim," Capital D told Mary-Kate and Ashley. They were in his studio the next day. "I'm even handsome when I'm wet!"

Ashley groaned softly. She and Mary-Kate didn't want to look through Capital D's photo album. They wanted to uncover his evil plan!

"Tell us about your music," Ashley said. "How do you make it play over everyone else's songs?"

"I don't want to bore you with details," Capital D replied. "Let's listen to my latest CD."

He pressed a button on a nearby stereo. A booming noise blasted from the speakers.

Quincy whined and tried to cover his ears.

"Quincy," Mary-Kate whispered. "Get Sammy Sam to leave the room. We'll find a way to lose Capital D. Then we can check out the sound equipment."

Ashley nodded. "Good idea," she said.

"You got it," Quincy answered. He barked like crazy and ran out of the room.

"Oh, no!" Ashley wailed. "We have to get our dog back!"

"Don't worry," Sammy Sam said. "I'll find him for you."

Sammy Sam ran after Quincy.

"Now to get rid of Capital D," Mary-Kate whispered to Ashley.

"Hey, what's that noise?" she said loudly. Mary-Kate winked at Ashley. Ashley knew that meant for her to play along.

"I don't know, but it sounds like . . . someone else's music!" Ashley added.

"What?" Capital D cried. "I don't hear it. Where is it coming from?"

"It sounds like it's coming from down the hall," Mary-Kate said. "You'd better go check it out!"

Capital D raced out of the room. The girls smiled at each other. Their plan had worked!

"This all looks pretty normal to me," Ashley said, examining the sound equipment.

"I think I know how Capital D controls the music," Mary-Kate said. She pulled a small red rod from her pocket.

"Is that an antenna?" Ashley asked.

Mary-Kate nodded. "I found it inside a speaker at the Funk Factory," she explained. "Thanks to IQ's X-ray headbands."

"Antennas are used to pick up sound waves," Ashley said. "So Capital D must plant these inside the clubs."

"Then he sends his music from

here," Mary-Kate went on. "And the antennas pick up the sound!"

The girls gave each other a high five.

"Congratulations," a mean-sounding voice said. "You figured it all out."

Mary-Kate and Ashley whirled around. Standing at the door was Sammy Sam. Standing next to him, holding Quincy, was Capital D. And they did *not* look happy.

Ashley gulped. They were caught!

"I heard you talking on my intercom
system," Capital D said. He reached out
and took the girls' special-agent
bracelets. Then he grabbed the
mini-antenna from Mary-Kate's hand.

"I thought you guys liked Capital D!" Sammy Sam said.

"How can anyone like a guy who makes you listen to his music?" Mary-Kate asked.

Capital D put a finger on a button in the wall. "Say good-bye, girls," he said.

Capital D pressed the button. The floor opened and Mary-Kate and Ashley started to fall!

"Auuuuggghhhh!" the girls screamed.

THUD! Ashley and Mary-Kate landed side by side on a small sofa.

"Check this place out," Mary-Kate whispered.

Ashley looked around the room. The walls were made of steel. There was an elevator at one end of the room and a door at the other.

"It's not very cozy," Ashley said.

The elevator doors opened. Capital D and Sammy Sam stepped out. The doors slammed shut behind them.

"Don't bother to call for help," Capital D said. "This is a soundproof room. No one can hear you."

"Why did you bring us here?" Mary-Kate asked.

"I'm going to make you stay and listen to my music," Capital D explained. "Until you like it!"

"Oh, great," Ashley said. What could be
worse than that?

Capital D walked over to the door. He
took out an electronic card and swiped it
through a high-tech lock. The light on the
lock flashed green. The door swung open.

"Enjoy the concert, girls!" Capital D laughed. He and Sammy Sam left the room.

Mary-Kate and Ashley ran for the door. But it closed too quickly. Capital D's music began to pound through the room.

"What do we do now?" Mary-Kate cried.

Ashley thought for a minute. Then she had an idea. "Mary-Kate, what if we can get Quincy to hear us?" she asked.

"How?" Mary-Kate replied. "This room is totally soundproof."

"Maybe not *totally*," Ashley said. "Really high-frequency sounds are so powerful that they can get through. And besides, dogs' ears are more sensitive than humans'."

"So Quincy might hear something we wouldn't?" Mary-Kate finished.

"Exactly," Ashley said.

"Ashley, all the random facts you know sure come in handy!" Mary-Kate said.

Ashley smiled. She loved collecting cool facts about all sorts of things. And she always seemed to use them on her missions!

Ashley looked around the room. "So what can we use to send out some high-frequency waves?" she asked.

"Well, since we know that they are high-pitched sounds," Mary-Kate said, "I think I have an idea."

She held out her hand. "Can I have one of your earrings?" she asked.

Ashley pulled off an earring. She handed it to Mary-Kate. Mary-Kate pulled a small mirror out of her pocket. She dragged the earring across the mirror. It made a horrible high-pitched noise.

"Ouch!" Ashley cried. The noise hurt her ears.

Mary-Kate pulled her X-ray headband over her eyes. She looked through the walls.

"What do you see?" Ashley asked.

"Quincy is right outside the door!" Mary-Kate exclaimed. "He's hitting the lock with his nose!"

BEEP! A second later the door flew open. Quincy bounded in.

"Quincy to the rescue!" Ashley cheered.

Mary-Kate and Ashley hugged Quincy. But they couldn't get warm and fuzzy for too long. They had a mission to complete!

CHAPTER SIX
An International Incident

Mary-Kate and Ashley raced through Capital D's studio.

"Look!" Ashley said. She pointed to two bracelets on Capital D's coffee table. "He left our bracelets here."

The girls grabbed them. Mary-Kate accidentally dropped hers on a nearby speaker.

SCREEEEEEECH! A high-pitched noise filled the room.

"Gee," Mary-Kate said. "I guess Capital D's speaker doesn't like my bracelet."

"We've got to move fast," Ashley warned. "The peace meeting starts in half an hour!"

The girls called Rod on their bracelets. He picked them up and took them to the meeting hall.

Ashley studied the guests as they entered the hall. Everyone was dressed in flowing gowns and fancy tuxedos!

"IQ arranged for us to DJ the party," Ashley whispered. "So it looks like we belong here."

Mary-Kate and Ashley squeezed through the crowd. They stopped near the stage. The leaders of each country stood proudly under their national flags.

"Just think," Mary-Kate said. "People from sixty-one nations are here in the same room."

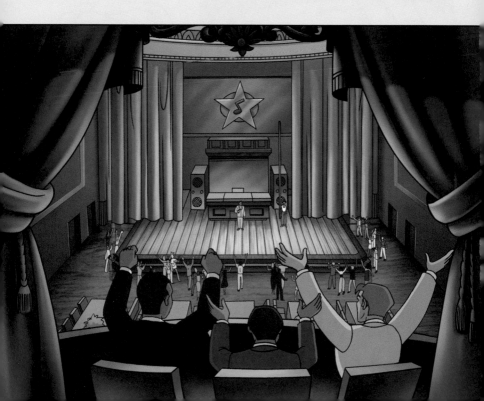

"And it looks like they're about to have some trouble!" Ashley whispered. She pointed backstage. Sammy Sam was sneaking toward the sound equipment.

"Uh-oh," Mary-Kate whispered. "We've got to stop him!"

Mary-Kate and Ashley raced backstage.

"How did you get out?" Sammy Sam cried when he saw them.

"That doesn't matter," Mary-Kate said. "All that matters is that we stop Capital D!"

"Don't mess things up," Sammy Sam pleaded. "Capital D just wants to spread his tunes worldwide. That's good, right?"

"What's good about hurting other people?" Mary-Kate asked. "Sixty-one countries want to hear their national anthems. Not Capital D's tunes!"

"Please tell us where Capital D is going to hide his antennas, Sammy Sam," Ashley begged.

She glanced onstage. She could see the French flag rising slowly into the air. France's national anthem began to play.

"Capital D already hid the antennas," Sammy Sam said. "He's at the studio getting ready to start his music."

"Oh, no!" Ashley cried. "That means that at any second—"

SCREECH! The French national anthem stopped playing. It was replaced with one of Capital D's tunes.

Ashley could hear the crowd's angry cries. "We'd better work fast," she said to Mary-Kate.

Mary-Kate and Ashley pulled the X-ray headbands over their eyes. They studied the insides of the sound equipment, looking for red antennas.

"Found one!" Ashley said. She pointed to a mini-antenna inside a speaker. "How do we stop it?"

"I know!" Mary-Kate said. "When I dropped my bracelet on Capital D's equipment, it gave off a high-pitched noise. It must mess with high-frequency sound waves."

"So maybe the bracelet will mess up the antenna!" Ashley said excitedly.

Mary-Kate removed her bracelet. She aimed it at the speaker. *POP!* The antenna crackled.

Capital D's song stopped playing. The French national anthem rang through the hall.

"Hooray!" the crowd cheered.

But a minute later Capital D's song was back!

"There must be tons of antennas back here," Ashley cried.

"And we have to find them fast," Mary-Kate said. "Or else the meeting will be ruined!"

CHAPTER SEVEN
The Peace Party

"There are only three antennas left,"
Sammy Sam chimed in.

Ashley turned to face Sammy Sam. He
was going to help them!

"One of the antennas is in here,"
Sammy Sam said. He pointed at a
speaker.

Ashley waved her bracelet in back of the speaker. The antenna popped. The French national anthem was back!

"You won't be sorry, Sammy Sam," Mary-Kate said.

"There's another antenna in that one," Sammy Sam said. He pointed across the room.

"Got it!" Mary-Kate said. She raced to the speaker.

"The last antenna is up there," Sammy Sam said. He pointed toward a small speaker at the top of a staircase.

"I'm on it!" Ashley said. She climbed the stairs and zapped the last antenna. Mission accomplished!

"Thanks, Sammy Sam," Mary-Kate said. "What made you decide to help us?"

"Seeing all those people out there made me think," Sammy Sam said. "Different people like different music."

"That's why it's not fair when one person tries to think for everybody else," Mary-Kate said.

"Just imagine how boring it would be if everybody liked all the same stuff!" Ashley exclaimed.

"But I thought Capital D's music would make everybody happy." Sammy Sam sighed. "I think he's awesome!"

"*You* think," Ashley pointed out. "That's cool for you. But somebody else might think some other music is awesome."

The French national anthem finished. The Chinese national anthem started up.

"IQ will be happy to hear how handy our X-ray headbands and special-agent bracelets were," Mary-Kate added.

Quincy walked backstage. "I told Headquarters what you found out," he said. "Teams are being sent to destroy antennas all over the country!"

"Whoa!" Sammy Sam gasped. "Your dog talks?"

"Quincy isn't just a dog," Ashley said. "He's a special agent. And so are we!"

"And now that the world is safe from Capital D's nasty noise," Mary-Kate said, "let's get this peace party started!"

"Right on, Sister Scarlet!" Ashley cheered.

Mary-Kate waited for the national anthems to stop playing. Then she grabbed the microphone and faced the crowd.

"Every one of us here is special," Mary-Kate said. "But there is room in the world for all our ideas, customs, habits, even music!"

"That's why we're here—to celebrate our differences," Ashley said. "And to party Sister Scarlet and Amber Jammer style!"

Mary-Kate pressed a few buttons on their DJ equipment. Soon the guests were dancing to the beat of Polyester Pal. Mary-Kate, Ashley, and Quincy started dancing, too.

"So are you ready for your test yet?" Quincy asked as he swayed back and forth.

"Are you kidding?" Ashley replied. She grinned. "We've got sound down to a *science*!"

FROM: Special Agents Misty and Amber
TO: All Mary-Kate and Ashley Fans
LOCATION: Everywhere

YOUR MISSION: Collect all the books in the series and join us as we save the world from super-villains who are out to cause trouble!

LET'S GO
SAVE THE WORLD...
AGAIN!

Find out what is causing the
fashion model meltdown!

Go undercover to solve
a sticky mess!

Stop the world from
turning into a desert!

Are the Hipslovian gymnasts
a perfect ten—or just
perfect cheaters?

Sniff out what's going
on at the Bot Puppy
factory!

COOL NEW BOOKS!

Can You Solve These Mysteries?

What happens when an ice cream thief tries to steal the secret recipe?

What happens to the prankster who wants to ruin Clue's circus act?

What happens when the mascot uniform disappears?

AVAILABLE WHEREVER BOOKS ARE SOLD

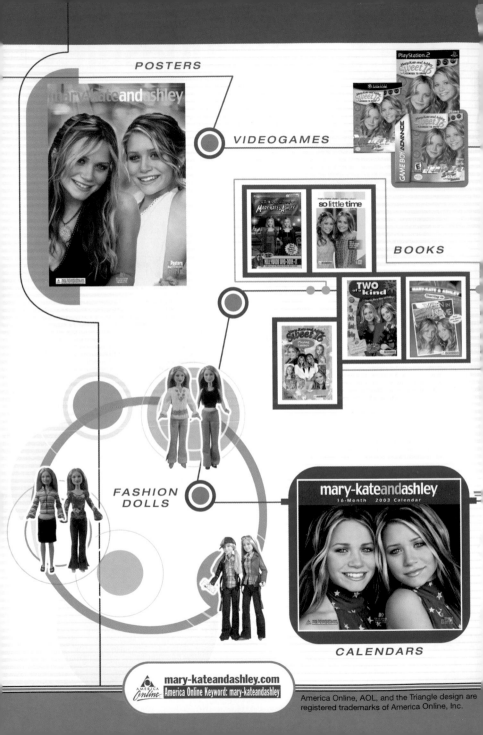

POSTERS

VIDEOGAMES

BOOKS

FASHION DOLLS

CALENDARS

mary-kate and ashley
16-Month 2003 Calendar